Marx Joyce
Defoe Abbott Hardy Machiavelli Chesterton Emerson Austen
Melville Montaigne Cooper Hugo Grimm
Haggard Eliot
Stoker Christie Molière
Wilde Carroll Byron Schiller
Maupassant Engels Smith Kafka
Garnett Fitzgerald Hawthorne Hall
Goethe Einstein Dostoyevsky Willis
Cotton Kipling Doyle
Baum Henry Nietzsche
Leslie Dumas Flaubert Turgenev Balzac
Stockton Vatsyayana Crane
Burroughs Verne
Curtis Tocqueville Gogol Vinci
Homer Widger Tolstoy Whitman Busch
Darwin Thoreau Twain
Potter Freud Zola Plato Scott Harte
Kant Jowett Lawrence Dickens Burton Hesse
Stevenson Cervantes
Andersen Voltaire
London Descartes Burton Cooke
Poe Aristotle Wells
Hale James Hastings Irving
Bunner Shakespeare
Richter Chambers Alcott
Doré da Shaw Benedict
Chekhov Wodehouse Pushkin
Swift Dante Newton

The Poetical Works of Oliver Wendell Holmes

Volume 9: the Iron Gate and Other Poems

Oliver Wendell Holmes

Imprint

This book is part of TREDITION CLASSICS

Author: Oliver Wendell Holmes
Cover design: Buchgut, Berlin – Germany

Publisher: tredition GmbH, Hamburg - Germany
ISBN: 978-3-8424-2996-3

www.tredition.com
www.tredition.de

THE POETICAL WORKS

OF

OLIVER WENDELL HOLMES

[Volume 3 of the 1893 three volume set]

THE IRON GATE

AND OTHER POEMS

1877-1881

THE IRON GATE

Read at the Breakfast given in honor of Dr. Holmes's Seventieth Birthday by the publishers of the "Atlantic Monthly," Boston, December 3, 1879.

WHERE is this patriarch you are kindly greeting?
Not unfamiliar to my ear his name,
Nor yet unknown to many a joyous meeting
In days long vanished, — is he still the same,

Or changed by years, forgotten and forgetting,
Dull-eared, dim-sighted, slow of speech and thought,
Still o'er the sad, degenerate present fretting,
Where all goes wrong, and nothing as it ought?

Old age, the graybeard! Well, indeed, I know him, —
Shrunk, tottering, bent, of aches and ills the prey;
In sermon, story, fable, picture, poem,
Oft have I met him from my earliest day.

In my old AEsop, toiling with his bundle, —
His load of sticks, — politely asking Death,
Who comes when called for, — would he lug or trundle
His fagot for him? — he was scant of breath.

And sad "Ecclesiastes, or the Preacher," —
Has he not stamped the image on my soul,
In that last chapter, where the worn-out Teacher
Sighs o'er the loosened cord, the broken bowl?

Yes, long, indeed, I've known him at a distance,
And now my lifted door-latch shows him here;
I take his shrivelled hand without resistance,
And find him smiling as his step draws near.

What though of gilded baubles he bereaves us,
Dear to the heart of youth, to manhood's prime;
Think of the calm he brings, the wealth he leaves us,
The hoarded spoils, the legacies of time!

Altars once flaming, still with incense fragrant,
Passion's uneasy nurslings rocked asleep,
Hope's anchor faster, wild desire less vagrant,
Life's flow less noisy, but the stream how deep!

Still as the silver cord gets worn and slender,
Its lightened task-work tugs with lessening strain,
Hands get more helpful, voices, grown more tender,
Soothe with their softened tones the slumberous brain.

Youth longs and manhood strives, but age remembers,
Sits by the raked-up ashes of the past,
Spreads its thin hands above the whitening embers
That warm its creeping life-blood till the last.

Dear to its heart is every loving token
That comes unbidden ere its pulse grows cold,
Ere the last lingering ties of life are broken,
Its labors ended and its story told.

Ah, while around us rosy youth rejoices,
For us the sorrow-laden breezes sigh,
And through the chorus of its jocund voices
Throbs the sharp note of misery's hopeless cry.

As on the gauzy wings of fancy flying
From some far orb I track our watery sphere,
Home of the struggling, suffering, doubting, dying,
The silvered globule seems a glistening tear.

But Nature lends her mirror of illusion
To win from saddening scenes our age-dimmed eyes,
And misty day-dreams blend in sweet confusion
The wintry landscape and the summer skies.

So when the iron portal shuts behind us,
And life forgets us in its noise and whirl,
Visions that shunned the glaring noonday find us,
And glimmering starlight shows the gates of pearl.

I come not here your morning hour to sadden,
A limping pilgrim, leaning on his staff, —
I, who have never deemed it sin to gladden
This vale of sorrows with a wholesome laugh.

If word of mine another's gloom has brightened,
Through my dumb lips the heaven-sent message came;
If hand of mine another's task has lightened,
It felt the guidance that it dares not claim.

But, O my gentle sisters, O my brothers,
These thick-sown snow-flakes hint of toil's release;
These feebler pulses bid me leave to others
The tasks once welcome; evening asks for peace.

Time claims his tribute; silence now is golden;
Let me not vex the too long suffering lyre;
Though to your love untiring still beholden,
The curfew tells me — cover up the fire.

And now with grateful smile and accents cheerful,
And warmer heart than look or word can tell,
In simplest phrase—these traitorous eyes are tearful—
Thanks, Brothers, Sisters,—Children,—and farewell!

VESTIGIA QUINQUE RETRORSUM

AN ACADEMIC POEM

1829-1879

Read at the Commencement Dinner of the Alumni of Harvard University, June 25, 1879.

WHILE fond, sad memories all around us throng,
Silence were sweeter than the sweetest song;
Yet when the leaves are green and heaven is blue,
The choral tribute of the grove is due,
And when the lengthening nights have chilled the skies,
We fain would hear the song-bird ere be flies,
And greet with kindly welcome, even as now,
The lonely minstrel on his leafless bough.

This is our golden year,—its golden day;
Its bridal memories soon must pass away;
Soon shall its dying music cease to ring,
And every year must loose some silver string,
Till the last trembling chords no longer thrill,—
Hands all at rest and hearts forever still.

A few gray heads have joined the forming line;
We hear our summons,—"Class of 'Twenty-Nine!"
Close on the foremost, and, alas, how few!

Are these "The Boys" our dear old Mother knew?
Sixty brave swimmers. Twenty — something more —
Have passed the stream and reached this frosty shore!

How near the banks these fifty years divide
When memory crosses with a single stride!
'T is the first year of stern "Old Hickory" 's rule
When our good Mother lets us out of school,
Half glad, half sorrowing, it must be confessed,
To leave her quiet lap, her bounteous breast,
Armed with our dainty, ribbon-tied degrees,
Pleased and yet pensive, exiles and A. B.'s.

Look back, O comrades, with your faded eyes,
And see the phantoms as I bid them rise.
Whose smile is that? Its pattern Nature gave,
A sunbeam dancing in a dimpled wave;
KIRKLAND alone such grace from Heaven could win,
His features radiant as the soul within;
That smile would let him through Saint Peter's gate
While sad-eyed martyrs had to stand and wait.
Here flits mercurial *Farrar*; standing there,
See mild, benignant, cautious, learned *Ware*,
And sturdy, patient, faithful, honest *Hedge*,
Whose grinding logic gave our wits their edge;
Ticknor, with honeyed voice and courtly grace;
And *Willard*, larynxed like a double bass;
And *Channing*, with his bland, superior look,
Cool as a moonbeam on a frozen brook,

While the pale student, shivering in his shoes,
Sees from his theme the turgid rhetoric ooze;
And the born soldier, fate decreed to wreak
His martial manhood on a class in Greek,
Popkin! How that explosive name recalls
The grand old Busby of our ancient halls
Such faces looked from Skippon's grim platoons,

Such figures rode with Ireton's stout dragoons:
He gave his strength to learning's gentle charms,
But every accent sounded "Shoulder arms!"

Names,—empty names! Save only here and there
Some white-haired listener, dozing in his chair,
Starts at the sound he often used to hear,
And upward slants his Sunday-sermon ear.
And we—our blooming manhood we regain;
Smiling we join the long Commencement train,
One point first battled in discussion hot,—
Shall we wear gowns? and settled: We will not.
How strange the scene,—that noisy boy-debate
Where embryo-speakers learn to rule the State!
This broad-browed youth, sedate and sober-eyed,
Shall wear the ermined robe at Taney's side;
And he, the stripling, smooth of face and slight,
Whose slender form scarce intercepts the light,
Shall rule the Bench where Parsons gave the law,
And sphinx-like sat uncouth, majestic Shaw
Ah, many a star has shed its fatal ray
On names we loved—our brothers—where are they?

Nor these alone; our hearts in silence claim
Names not less dear, unsyllabled by fame.

How brief the space! and yet it sweeps us back
Far, far along our new-born history's track
Five strides like this;—the sachem rules the land;
The Indian wigwams cluster where we stand.

The second. Lo! a scene of deadly strife—
A nation struggling into infant life;
Not yet the fatal game at Yorktown won
Where failing Empire fired its sunset gun.
LANGDON sits restless in the ancient chair,—
Harvard's grave Head,—these echoes heard his prayer

When from yon mansion, dear to memory still,
The banded yeomen marched for Bunker's Hill.
Count on the grave triennial's thick-starred roll
What names were numbered on the lengthening scroll, —
Not unfamiliar in our ears they ring, —
Winthrop, Hale, Eliot, Everett, Dexter, Tyng.

Another stride. Once more at 'twenty-nine, —
GOD SAVE KING GEORGE, the Second of his line!
And is Sir Isaac living? Nay, not so, —
He followed Flainsteed two short years ago, —
And what about the little hump-backed man
Who pleased the bygone days of good Queen Anne?
What, Pope? another book he's just put out, —
"The Dunciad," — witty, but profane, no doubt.

Where's Cotton Mather? he was always here.
And so he would be, but he died last year.
Who is this preacher our Northampton claims,
Whose rhetoric blazes with sulphureous flames
And torches stolen from Tartarean mines?
Edwards, the salamander of divines.
A deep, strong nature, pure and undefiled;
Faith, firm as his who stabbed his sleeping child;
Alas for him who blindly strays apart,
And seeking God has lost his human heart!
Fall where they might, no flying cinders caught
These sober halls where WADSWORTH ruled and
taught.

One footstep more; the fourth receding stride
Leaves the round century on the nearer side.
GOD SAVE KING CHARLES! God knows that pleasant knave
His grace will find it hard enough to save.
Ten years and more, and now the Plague, the Fire,
Talk of all tongues, at last begin to tire;
One fear prevails, all other frights forgot, —

White lips are whispering, — hark! The Popish Plot!
Happy New England, from such troubles free
In health and peace beyond the stormy sea!
No Romish daggers threat her children's throats,
No gibbering nightmare mutters "Titus Oates;"
Philip is slain, the Quaker graves are green,
Not yet the witch has entered on the scene;
Happy our Harvard; pleased her graduates four;
URIAN OAKES the name their parchments bore.

Two centuries past, our hurried feet arrive
At the last footprint of the scanty five;
Take the fifth stride; our wandering eyes explore
A tangled forest on a trackless shore;
Here, where we stand, the savage sorcerer howls,
The wild cat snarls, the stealthy gray wolf prowls,
The slouching bear, perchance the trampling moose
Starts the brown squaw and scares her red pappoose;
At every step the lurking foe is near;
His Demons reign; God has no temple here!

Lift up your eyes! behold these pictured walls;
Look where the flood of western glory falls
Through the great sunflower disk of blazing panes
In ruby, saffron, azure, emerald stains;
With reverent step the marble pavement tread
Where our proud Mother's martyr-roll is read;
See the great halls that cluster, gathering round
This lofty shrine with holiest memories crowned;
See the fair Matron in her summer bower,
Fresh as a rose in bright perennial flower;
Read on her standard, always in the van,
"TRUTH," — the one word that makes a slave a man;
Think whose the hands that fed her altar-fires,
Then count the debt we owe our scholar-sires!

Brothers, farewell! the fast declining ray
Fades to the twilight of our golden day;
Some lesson yet our wearied brains may learn,
Some leaves, perhaps, in life's thin volume turn.
How few they seem as in our waning age
We count them backwards to the title-page!
Oh let us trust with holy men of old
Not all the story here begun is told;
So the tired spirit, waiting to be freed,
On life's last leaf with tranquil eye shall read
By the pale glimmer of the torch reversed,
Not Finis, but *The End of Volume First*!

MY AVIARY

Through my north window, in the wintry weather, —
My airy oriel on the river shore, —
I watch the sea-fowl as they flock together
Where late the boatman flashed his dripping oar.

The gull, high floating, like a sloop unladen,
Lets the loose water waft him as it will;
The duck, round-breasted as a rustic maiden,
Paddles and plunges, busy, busy still.

I see the solemn gulls in council sitting
On some broad ice-floe pondering long and late,
While overhead the home-bound ducks are flitting,
And leave the tardy conclave in debate,

Those weighty questions in their breasts revolving
Whose deeper meaning science never learns,

Till at some reverend elder's look dissolving,
The speechless senate silently adjourns.

But when along the waves the shrill north-easter
Shrieks through the laboring coaster's shrouds "Beware!"
The pale bird, kindling like a Christmas feaster
When some wild chorus shakes the vinous air,

Flaps from the leaden wave in fierce rejoicing,
Feels heaven's dumb lightning thrill his torpid nerves,
Now on the blast his whistling plumage poising,
Now wheeling, whirling in fantastic curves.

Such is our gull; a gentleman of leisure,
Less fleshed than feathered; bagged you'll find him such;
His virtue silence; his employment pleasure;
Not bad to look at, and not good for much.

What of our duck? He has some high-bred cousins, —
His Grace the Canvas-back, My Lord the Brant, —
Anas and Anser, — both served up by dozens,
At Boston's Rocher, half-way to Nahant.

As for himself, he seems alert and thriving, —
Grubs up a living somehow — what, who knows?
Crabs? mussels? weeds? — Look quick! there 's one just diving!
Flop! Splash! his white breast glistens — down he goes!

And while he 's under — just about a minute —
I take advantage of the fact to say
His fishy carcase has no virtue in it
The gunning idiot's worthless hire to pay.

Shrewd is our bird; not easy to outwit him!
Sharp is the outlook of those pin-head eyes;

Still, he is mortal and a shot may hit him,
One cannot always miss him if he tries.

He knows you! "sportsmen" from suburban alleys,
Stretched under seaweed in the treacherous punt;
Knows every lazy, shiftless lout that sallies
Forth to waste powder—as he says, to "hunt."

I watch you with a patient satisfaction,
Well pleased to discount your predestined luck;
The float that figures in your sly transaction
Will carry back a goose, but not a duck.

Look! there's a young one, dreaming not of danger;
Sees a flat log come floating down the stream;
Stares undismayed upon the harmless stranger;
Ah! were all strangers harmless as they seem!

Habet! a leaden shower his breast has shattered;
Vainly he flutters, not again to rise;
His soft white plumes along the waves are scattered;
Helpless the wing that braved the tempest lies.

He sees his comrades high above him flying
To seek their nests among the island reeds;
Strong is their flight; all lonely he is lying
Washed by the crimsoned water as he bleeds.

O Thou who carest for the falling sparrow,
Canst Thou the sinless sufferer's pang forget?
Or is thy dread account-book's page so narrow
Its one long column scores thy creatures' debt?

Poor gentle guest, by nature kindly cherished,
A world grows dark with thee in blinding death;

One little gasp—thy universe has perished,
Wrecked by the idle thief who stole thy breath!

Is this the whole sad story of creation,
Lived by its breathing myriads o'er and o'er,—
One glimpse of day, then black annihilation,—
A sunlit passage to a sunless shore?

Give back our faith, ye mystery-solving lynxes!
Robe us once more in heaven-aspiring creeds
Happier was dreaming Egypt with her sphinxes,
The stony convent with its cross and beads!

How often gazing where a bird reposes,
Rocked on the wavelets, drifting with the tide,
I lose myself in strange metempsychosis
And float a sea-fowl at a sea-fowl's side;

From rain, hail, snow in feathery mantle muffled,
Clear-eyed, strong-limbed, with keenest sense to hear
My mate soft murmuring, who, with plumes unruffled,
Where'er I wander still is nestling near;

The great blue hollow like a garment o'er me;
Space all unmeasured, unrecorded time;
While seen with inward eye moves on before me
Thought's pictured train in wordless pantomime.

A voice recalls me.—From my window turning
I find myself a plumeless biped still;
No beak, no claws, no sign of wings discerning,—
In fact with nothing bird-like but my quill.

ON THE THRESHOLD

INTRODUCTION TO A COLLECTION OF POEMS BYDIFFER-ENT AUTHORS

AN usher standing at the door
I show my white rosette;
A smile of welcome, nothing more,
Will pay my trifling debt;
Why should I bid you idly wait
Like lovers at the swinging gate?

Can I forget the wedding guest?
The veteran of the sea?
In vain the listener smites his breast, —
"There was a ship," cries he!
Poor fasting victim, stunned and pale,
IIe needs must listen to the tale.

He sees the gilded throng within,
The sparkling goblets gleam,
The music and the merry din
Through every window stream,
But there he shivers in the cold
Till all the crazy dream is told.

Not mine the graybeard's glittering eye
That held his captive still
To hold my silent prisoners by
And let me have my will;
Nay, I were like the three-years' child,
To think you could be so beguiled!

My verse is but the curtain's fold
That hides the painted scene,
The mist by morning's ray unrolled
That veils the meadow's green,

The cloud that needs must drift away
To show the rose of opening day.

See, from the tinkling rill you hear
In hollowed palm I bring
These scanty drops, but ah, how near
The founts that heavenward spring!
Thus, open wide the gates are thrown
And founts and flowers are all your own!

TO GEORGE PEABODY

DANVERS, 1866

BANKRUPT! our pockets inside out!
Empty of words to speak his praises!
Worcester and Webster up the spout!
Dead broke of laudatory phrases!
Yet why with flowery speeches tease,
With vain superlatives distress him?
Has language better words than these?
THE FRIEND OF ALL HIS RACE, GOD BLESS HIM!

A simple prayer — but words more sweet
By human lips were never uttered,
Since Adam left the country seat
Where angel wings around him fluttered.
The old look on with tear-dimmed eyes,
The children cluster to caress him,
And every voice unbidden cries,
THE FRIEND OF ALL HIS RACE, GOD BLESS HIM!

AT THE PAPYRUS CLUB

A LOVELY show for eyes to see
I looked upon this morning, —
A bright-hued, feathered company
Of nature's own adorning;
But ah! those minstrels would not sing
A listening ear while I lent, —
The lark sat still and preened his wing,
The nightingale was silent;
I longed for what they gave me not —
Their warblings sweet and fluty,
But grateful still for all I got
I thanked them for their beauty.

A fairer vision meets my view
Of Claras, Margarets, Marys,
In silken robes of varied hue,
Like bluebirds and canaries;
The roses blush, the jewels gleam,
The silks and satins glisten,
The black eyes flash, the blue eyes beam,
We look — and then we listen
Behold the flock we cage to-night —
Was ever such a capture?
To see them is a pure delight;
To hear them — ah! what rapture!

Methinks I hear Delilah's laugh
At Samson bound in fetters;
"We captured!" shrieks each lovelier half,
"Men think themselves our betters!
We push the bolt, we turn the key
On warriors, poets, sages,
Too happy, all of them, to be
Locked in our golden cages!"
Beware! the boy with bandaged eyes

Has flung away his blinder;

He 's lost his mother — so he cries —
And here he knows he'll find her:
The rogue! 't is but a new device, —
Look out for flying arrows
Whene'er the birds of Paradise
Are perched amid the sparrows!

FOR WHITTIER'S SEVENTIETH BIRTHDAY

DECEMBER 17, 1877

I BELIEVE that the copies of verses I've spun,
Like Scheherezade's tales, are a thousand and one;
You remember the story, — those mornings in bed, —
'T was the turn of a copper, — a tale or a head.

A doom like Scheherezade's falls upon me
In a mandate as stern as the Sultan's decree
I'm a florist in verse, and what would people say
If I came to a banquet without my bouquet?

It is trying, no doubt, when the company knows
Just the look and the smell of each lily and rose,
The green of each leaf in the sprigs that I bring,
And the shape of the bunch and the knot of the string.

Yes, — "the style is the man," and the nib of one's pen
Makes the same mark at twenty, and threescore and ten;
It is so in all matters, if truth may be told;

Let one look at the cast he can tell you the mould.

How we all know each other! no use in disguise;
Through the holes in the mask comes the flash of the eyes;
We can tell by his — somewhat — each one of our tribe,
As we know the old hat which we cannot describe.

Though in Hebrew, in Sanscrit, in Choctaw you write,
Sweet singer who gave us the Voices of Night,
Though in buskin or slipper your song may be shod;
Or the velvety verse that Evangeline trod,

We shall say, "You can't cheat us, — we know it is you,"
There is one voice like that, but there cannot be two,
Maestro, whose chant like the dulcimer rings
And the woods will be hushed while the nightingale sings.

And he, so serene, so majestic, so true,
Whose temple hypethral the planets shine through,
Let us catch but five words from that mystical pen,
We should know our one sage from all children of men.

And he whose bright image no distance can dim,
Through a hundred disguises we can't mistake him,
Whose play is all earnest, whose wit is the edge
(With a beetle behind) of a sham-splitting wedge.

Do you know whom we send you, Hidalgos of Spain?
Do you know your old friends when you see them again?
Hosea was Sancho! you Dons of Madrid,
But Sancho that wielded the lance of the Cid!

And the wood-thrush of Essex, — you know whom I mean,
Whose song echoes round us while he sits unseen,
Whose heart-throbs of verse through our memories thrill

Like a breath from the wood, like a breeze from the hill,

So fervid, so simple, so loving, so pure,
We hear but one strain and our verdict is sure, —
Thee cannot elude us, — no further we search, —
'T is Holy George Herbert cut loose from his church!

We think it the voice of a seraph that sings, —
Alas! we remember that angels have wings, —
What story is this of the day of his birth?
Let him live to a hundred! we want him on earth!

One life has been paid him (in gold) by the sun;
One account has been squared and another begun;
But he never will die if he lingers below
Till we've paid him in love half the balance we owe!

TWO SONNETS: HARVARD

At the meeting of the New York Harvard Club,
February 21, 1878.

"CHRISTO ET ECCLESLE." 1700

To GOD'S ANOINTED AND HIS CHOSEN FLOCK
So ran the phrase the black-robed conclave chose
To guard the sacred cloisters that arose
Like David's altar on Moriah's rock.
Unshaken still those ancient arches mock
The ram's-horn summons of the windy foes
Who stand like Joshua's army while it blows
And wait to see them toppling with the shock.

Christ and the Church. Their church, whose narrow door
Shut out the many, who if overbold
Like hunted wolves were driven from the fold,
Bruised with the flails these godly zealots bore,
Mindful that Israel's altar stood of old
Where echoed once Araunah's threshing-floor.

1643 "VERITAS." 1878

TRUTH: So the frontlet's older legend ran,
On the brief record's opening page displayed;
Not yet those clear-eyed scholars were afraid
Lest the fair fruit that wrought the woe of man
By far Euphrates—where our sire began
His search for truth, and, seeking, was betrayed—
Might work new treason in their forest shade,
Doubling the curse that brought life's shortened span.
Nurse of the future, daughter of the past,
That stern phylactery best becomes thee now
Lift to the morning star thy marble brow
Cast thy brave truth on every warring blast!
Stretch thy white hand to that forbidden bough,
And let thine earliest symbol be thy last!

THE COMING ERA

THEY tell us that the Muse is soon to fly hence,
Leaving the bowers of song that once were dear,
Her robes bequeathing to her sister, Science,
The groves of Pindus for the axe to clear.

Optics will claim the wandering eye of fancy,
Physics will grasp imagination's wings,
Plain fact exorcise fiction's necromancy,
The workshop hammer where the minstrel sings,

No more with laugher at Thalia's frolics
Our eyes shall twinkle till the tears run down,
But in her place the lecturer on hydraulics
Spout forth his watery science to the town.

No more our foolish passions and affections
The tragic Muse with mimic grief shall try,
But, nobler far, a course of vivisections
Teach what it costs a tortured brute to die.

The unearthed monad, long in buried rocks hid,
Shall tell the secret whence our being came;
The chemist show us death is life's black oxide,
Left when the breath no longer fans its flame.

Instead of crack-brained poets in their attics
Filling thin volumes with their flowery talk,
There shall be books of wholesome mathematics;
The tutor with his blackboard and his chalk.

No longer bards with madrigal and sonnet
Shall woo to moonlight walks the ribboned sex,
But side by side the beaver and the bonnet
Stroll, calmly pondering on some problem's x.

The sober bliss of serious calculation
Shall mock the trivial joys that fancy drew,
And, oh, the rapture of a solved equation,—
One self-same answer on the lips of two!

So speak in solemn tones our youthful sages,
Patient, severe, laborious, slow, exact,
As o'er creation's protoplasmic pages
They browse and munch the thistle crops of fact.

And yet we 've sometimes found it rather pleasant
To dream again the scenes that Shakespeare drew, —
To walk the hill-side with the Scottish peasant
Among the daisies wet with morning's dew;

To leave awhile the daylight of the real,
Led by the guidance of the master's hand,
For the strange radiance of the far ideal, —
"The light that never was on sea or land."

Well, Time alone can lift the future's curtain, —
Science may teach our children all she knows,
But Love will kindle fresh young hearts, 't is certain,
And June will not forget her blushing rose.

And so, in spite of all that Time is bringing, —
Treasures of truth and miracles of art,
Beauty and Love will keep the poet singing,
And song still live, the science of the heart.

IN RESPONSE

Breakfast at the Century Club, New York, May, 1879.

SUCH kindness! the scowl of a cynic would soften,
His pulse beat its way to some eloquent words,
Alas! my poor accents have echoed too often,

Like that Pinafore music you've some of you heard.

Do you know me, dear strangers — the hundredth time comer
At banquets and feasts since the days of my Spring?
Ah! would I could borrow one rose of my Summer,
But this is a leaf of my Autumn I bring.

I look at your faces, — I'm sure there are some from
The three-breasted mother I count as my own;
You think you remember the place you have come from,
But how it has changed in the years that have flown!

Unaltered, 't is true, is the hall we call "Funnel,"
Still fights the "Old South" in the battle for life,
But we've opened our door to the West through the tunnel,
And we've cut off Fort Hill with our Amazon knife.

You should see the new Westminster Boston has builded, —
Its mansions, its spires, its museums of arts, —
You should see the great dome we have gorgeously gilded, —
'T is the light of our eyes, 't is the joy of our hearts.

When first in his path a young asteroid found it,
As he sailed through the skies with the stars in his wake,
He thought 't was the sun, and kept circling around it
Till Edison signalled, "You've made a mistake."

We are proud of our city, — her fast-growing figure,
The warp and the woof of her brain and her hands, —
But we're proudest of all that her heart has grown bigger,
And warms with fresh blood as her girdle expands.

One lesson the rubric of conflict has taught her
Though parted awhile by war's earth-rending shock,

The lines that divide us are written in water,
The love that unites us cut deep in the rock.

As well might the Judas of treason endeavor
To write his black name on the disk of the sun
As try the bright star-wreath that binds us to sever
And blot the fair legend of "Many in One."

We love You, tall sister, the stately, the splendid, —
The banner of empire floats high on your towers,
Yet ever in welcome your arms are extended, —
We share in your splendors, your glory is ours.

Yes, Queen of the Continent! All of us own thee, —
The gold-freighted argosies flock at thy call,
The naiads, the sea-nymphs have met to enthrone thee,
But the Broadway of one is the Highway of all!

I thank you. Three words that can hardly be mended,
Though phrases on phrases their eloquence pile,
If you hear the heart's throb with their eloquence blended,
And read all they mean in a sunshiny smile.

FOR THE MOORE CENTENNIAL CELEBRATION

MAY 28, 1879.

ENCHANTER of Erin, whose magic has bound us,
Thy wand for one moment we fondly would claim,
Entranced while it summons the phantoms around us
That blush into life at the sound of thy name.

The tell-tales of memory wake from their slumbers, —
I hear the old song with its tender refrain, —
What passion lies hid in those honey-voiced numbers
What perfume of youth in each exquisite strain!

The home of my childhood comes back as a vision, —
Hark! Hark! A soft chord from its song-haunted room, —
'T is a morning of May, when the air is Elysian, —
The syringa in bud and the lilac in bloom, —

We are clustered around the "Clementi" piano, —
There were six of us then, — there are two of us now, —
She is singing — the girl with the silver soprano —
How "The Lord of the Valley" was false to his vow;

"Let Erin remember" the echoes are calling;
Through "The Vale of Avoca" the waters are rolled;
"The Exile" laments while the night-dews falling;
"The Morning of Life" dawns again as of old.

But ah! those warm love-songs of fresh adolescence!
Around us such raptures celestial they flung
That it seemed as if Paradise breathed its quintessence
Through the seraph-toned lips of the maiden that sung!

Long hushed are the chords that my boyhood enchanted
As when the smooth wave by the angel was stirred,
Yet still with their music is memory haunted,
And oft in my dreams are their melodies heard.

I feel like the priest to his altar returning, —
The crowd that was kneeling no longer is there,
The flame has died down, but the brands are still burning,
And sandal and cinnamon sweeten the air.

II.
The veil for her bridal young Summer is weaving
In her azure-domed hall with its tapestried floor,
And Spring the last tear-drop of May-dew is leaving
On the daisy of Burns and the shamrock of Moore.

How like, how unlike, as we view them together,
The song of the minstrels whose record we scan, —
One fresh as the breeze blowing over the heather,
One sweet as the breath from an odalisque's fan!

Ah, passion can glow mid a palace's splendor;
The cage does not alter the song of the bird;
And the curtain of silk has known whispers as tender
As ever the blossoming hawthorn has heard.

No fear lest the step of the soft-slippered Graces
Should fright the young Loves from their warm little nest,
For the heart of a queen, under jewels and laces,
Beats time with the pulse in the peasant girl's breast!

Thrice welcome each gift of kind Nature's bestowing!
Her fountain heeds little the goblet we hold;
Alike, when its musical waters are flowing,
The shell from the seaside, the chalice of gold.

The twins of the lyre to her voices had listened;
Both laid their best gifts upon Liberty's shrine;
For Coila's loved minstrel the holly-wreath glistened;
For Erin's the rose and the myrtle entwine.

And while the fresh blossoms of summer are braided
For the sea-girdled, stream-silvered, lake-jewelled isle,
While her mantle of verdure is woven unfaded,
While Shannon and Liffey shall dimple and smile,

The land where the staff of Saint Patrick was planted,
Where the shamrock grows green from the cliffs to the shore,
The land of fair maidens and heroes undaunted,
Shall wreathe her bright harp with the garlands of Moore!

TO JAMES FREEMAN CLARKE

APRIL 4, 1880

I BRING the simplest pledge of love,
Friend of my earlier days;
Mine is the hand without the glove,
The heart-beat, not the phrase.

How few still breathe this mortal air
We called by school-boy names!
You still, whatever robe you wear,
To me are always James.

That name the kind apostle bore
Who shames the sullen creeds,
Not trusting less, but loving more,
And showing faith by deeds.

What blending thoughts our memories share!
What visions yours and mine
Of May-days in whose morning air
The dews were golden wine,

Of vistas bright with opening day,
Whose all-awakening sun
Showed in life's landscape, far away,

The summits to be won!

The heights are gained. Ah, say not so
For him who smiles at time,
Leaves his tired comrades down below,
And only lives to climb!

His labors,—will they ever cease,—
With hand and tongue and pen?
Shall wearied Nature ask release
At threescore years and ten?

Our strength the clustered seasons tax,—
For him new life they mean;
Like rods around the lictor's axe
They keep him bright and keen.

The wise, the brave, the strong, we know,—
We mark them here or there,
But he,—we roll our eyes, and lo!
We find him everywhere!

With truth's bold cohorts, or alone,
He strides through error's field;
His lance is ever manhood's own,
His breast is woman's shield.

Count not his years while earth has need
Of souls that Heaven inflames
With sacred zeal to save, to lead,—
Long live our dear Saint James!

WELCOME TO THE CHICAGO COMMERCIAL CLUB

January 14, 1880

CHICAGO sounds rough to the maker of verse;
One comfort we have—Cincinnati sounds worse;
If we only were licensed to say Chicago!
But Worcester and Webster won't let us, you know.

No matter, we songsters must sing as we can;
We can make some nice couplets with Lake Michigan,
And what more resembles a nightingale's voice,
Than the oily trisyllable, sweet Illinois?

Your waters are fresh, while our harbor is salt,
But we know you can't help it—it is n't your fault;
Our city is old and your city is new,
But the railroad men tell us we're greener than you.

You have seen our gilt dome, and no doubt you've been told
That the orbs of the universe round it are rolled;
But I'll own it to you, and I ought to know best,
That this is n't quite true of all stars of the West.

You'll go to Mount Auburn,—we'll show you the track,—
And can stay there,—unless you prefer to come back;
And Bunker's tall shaft you can climb if you will,
But you'll puff like a paragraph praising a pill.

You must see—but you have seen—our old Faneuil Hall,
Our churches, our school-rooms, our sample-rooms, all;
And, perhaps, though the idiots must have their jokes,
You have found our good people much like other folks.

There are cities by rivers, by lakes, and by seas,
Each as full of itself as a cheese-mite of cheese;
And a city will brag as a game-cock will crow

Don't your cockerels at home—just a little, you know?

But we'll crow for you now—here's a health to the boys,
Men, maidens, and matrons of fair Illinois,
And the rainbow of friendship that arches its span
From the green of the sea to the blue Michigan!

AMERICAN ACADEMY CENTENNIAL CELEBRA-TION

MAY 26, 1880

SIRE, son, and grandson; so the century glides;
Three lives, three strides, three foot-prints in the sand;
Silent as midnight's falling meteor slides
Into the stillness of the far-off land;
How dim the space its little arc has spanned!

See on this opening page the names renowned
Tombed in these records on our dusty shelves,
Scarce on the scroll of living memory found,
Save where the wan-eyed antiquarian delves;
Shadows they seem; ab, what are we ourselves?

Pale ghosts of Bowdoin, Winthrop, Willard, West,
Sages of busy brain and wrinkled brow,
Searchers of Nature's secrets unconfessed,
Asking of all things Whence and Why and How—
What problems meet your larger vision now?

Has Gannett tracked the wild Aurora's path?
Has Bowdoin found his all-surrounding sphere?

What question puzzles ciphering Philomath?
Could Williams make the hidden causes clear
Of the Dark Day that filled the land with fear?

Dear ancient school-boys! Nature taught to them
The simple lessons of the star and flower,
Showed them strange sights; how on a single stem, —
Admire the marvels of Creative Power! —
Twin apples grew, one sweet, the other sour;

How from the hill-top where our eyes beheld
In even ranks the plumed and bannered maize
Range its long columns, in the days of old
The live volcano shot its angry blaze, —
Dead since the showers of Noah's watery days;

How, when the lightning split the mighty rock,
The spreading fury of the shaft was spent!
How the young scion joined the alien stock,
And when and where the homeless swallows went
To pass the winter of their discontent.

Scant were the gleanings in those years of dearth;
No Cuvier yet had clothed the fossil bones
That slumbered, waiting for their second birth;
No Lyell read the legend of the stones;
Science still pointed to her empty thrones.

Dreaming of orbs to eyes of earth unknown,
Herschel looked heavenwards in the starlight pale;
Lost in those awful depths he trod alone,
Laplace stood mute before the lifted veil;
While home-bred Humboldt trimmed his toy ship's sail.

No mortal feet these loftier heights had gained
Whence the wide realms of Nature we descry;

In vain their eyes our longing fathers strained
To scan with wondering gaze the summits high
That far beneath their children's footpaths lie.

Smile at their first small ventures as we may,
The school-boy's copy shapes the scholar's hand,
Their grateful memory fills our hearts to-day;
Brave, hopeful, wise, this bower of peace they planned,
While war's dread ploughshare scarred the suffering land.

Child of our children's children yet unborn,
When on this yellow page you turn your eyes,
Where the brief record of this May-day morn
In phrase antique and faded letters lies,
How vague, how pale our flitting ghosts will rise!

Yet in our veins the blood ran warm and red,
For us the fields were green, the skies were blue,
Though from our dust the spirit long has fled,
We lived, we loved, we toiled, we dreamed like you,
Smiled at our sires and thought how much we knew.

Oh might our spirits for one hour return,
When the next century rounds its hundredth ring,
All the strange secrets it shall teach to learn,
To hear the larger truths its years shall bring,
Its wiser sages talk, its sweeter minstrels sing!

THE SCHOOL-BOY

Read at the Centennial Celebration of the foundation of Phillips
Academy, Andover.

1778-1878

THESE hallowed precincts, long to memory dear,
Smile with fresh welcome as our feet draw near;
With softer gales the opening leaves are fanned,
With fairer hues the kindling flowers expand,
The rose-bush reddens with the blush of June,
The groves are vocal with their minstrels' tune,
The mighty elm, beneath whose arching shade
The wandering children of the forest strayed,
Greets the bright morning in its bridal dress,
And spreads its arms the gladsome dawn to bless.
Is it an idle dream that nature shares
Our joys, our griefs, our pastimes, and our cares?
Is there no summons when, at morning's call,
The sable vestments of the darkness fall?
Does not meek evening's low-voiced Ave blend
With the soft vesper as its notes ascend?
Is there no whisper in the perfumed air
When the sweet bosom of the rose is bare?
Does not the sunshine call us to rejoice?
Is there no meaning in the storm-cloud's voice?
No silent message when from midnight skies
Heaven looks upon us with its myriad eyes?

Or shift the mirror; say our dreams diffuse
O'er life's pale landscape their celestial hues,
Lend heaven the rainbow it has never known,
And robe the earth in glories not its own,
Sing their own music in the summer breeze,
With fresher foliage clothe the stately trees,
Stain the June blossoms with a livelier dye
And spread a bluer azure on the sky, —
Blest be the power that works its lawless will
And finds the weediest patch an Eden still;
No walls so fair as those our fancies build, —
No views so bright as those our visions gild!

So ran my lines, as pen and paper met,
The truant goose-quill travelling like Planchette;
Too ready servant, whose deceitful ways
Full many a slipshod line, alas! betrays;
Hence of the rhyming thousand not a few
Have builded worse — a great deal — than they knew.

What need of idle fancy to adorn
Our mother's birthplace on her birthday morn?
Hers are the blossoms of eternal spring,
From these green boughs her new-fledged birds take wing,
These echoes hear their earliest carols sung,
In this old nest the brood is ever young.
If some tired wanderer, resting from his flight,
Amid the gay young choristers alight,
These gather round him, mark his faded plumes
That faintly still the far-off grove perfumes,
And listen, wondering if some feeble note
Yet lingers, quavering in his weary throat: —
I, whose fresh voice yon red-faced temple knew,
What tune is left me, fit to sing to you?
Ask not the grandeurs of a labored song,
But let my easy couplets slide along;
Much could I tell you that you know too well;
Much I remember, but I will not tell;
Age brings experience; graybeards oft are wise,
But oh! how sharp a youngster's ears and eyes!

My cheek was bare of adolescent down
When first I sought the academic town;
Slow rolls the coach along the dusty road,
Big with its filial and parental load;
The frequent hills, the lonely woods are past,
The school-boy's chosen home is reached at last.
I see it now, the same unchanging spot,
The swinging gate, the little garden plot,
The narrow yard, the rock that made its floor,
The flat, pale house, the knocker-garnished door,

The small, trim parlor, neat, decorous, chill,
The strange, new faces, kind, but grave and still;
Two, creased with age, — or what I then called age, —
Life's volume open at its fiftieth page;
One, a shy maiden's, pallid, placid, sweet
As the first snow-drop, which the sunbeams greet;
One, the last nursling's; slight she was, and fair,
Her smooth white forehead warmed with auburn hair;
Last came the virgin Hymen long had spared,
Whose daily cares the grateful household shared,
Strong, patient, humble; her substantial frame
Stretched the chaste draperies I forbear to name.
Brave, but with effort, had the school-boy come
To the cold comfort of a stranger's home;
How like a dagger to my sinking heart
Came the dry summons, "It is time to part;
Good-by!" "Goo-ood-by!" one fond maternal kiss. . . .
Homesick as death! Was ever pang like this?
Too young as yet with willing feet to stray
From the tame fireside, glad to get away, —
Too old to let my watery grief appear, —
And what so bitter as a swallowed tear!
One figure still my vagrant thoughts pursue;
First boy to greet me, Ariel, where are you?
Imp of all mischief, heaven alone knows how
You learned it all, — are you an angel now,
Or tottering gently down the slope of years,
Your face grown sober in the vale of tears?
Forgive my freedom if you are breathing still;

If in a happier world, I know you will.
You were a school-boy — what beneath the sun
So like a monkey? I was also one.
Strange, sure enough, to see what curious shoots
The nursery raises from the study's roots!
In those old days the very, very good
Took up more room — a little — than they should;
Something too much one's eyes encountered then

Of serious youth and funeral-visaged men;
The solemn elders saw life's mournful half,—
Heaven sent this boy, whose mission was to laugh,
Drollest of buffos, Nature's odd protest,
A catbird squealing in a blackbird's nest.
Kind, faithful Nature! While the sour-eyed Scot—
Her cheerful smiles forbidden or forgot—
Talks only of his preacher and his kirk,—
Hears five-hour sermons for his Sunday work,—
Praying and fasting till his meagre face
Gains its due length, the genuine sign of grace,—
An Ayrshire mother in the land of Knox
Her embryo poet in his cradle rocks;—
Nature, long shivering in her dim eclipse,
Steals in a sunbeam to those baby lips;
So to its home her banished smile returns,
And Scotland sweetens with the song of Burns!

The morning came; I reached the classic hall;
A clock-face eyed me, staring from the wall;
Beneath its hands a printed line I read
YOUTH IS LIFE'S SEED-TIME: so the clock-face said:
Some took its counsel, as the sequel showed,—
Sowed,—their wild oats,—and reaped as they had sowed.
How all comes back! the upward slanting floor,—
The masters' thrones that flank the central door,—
The long, outstretching alleys that divide
The rows of desks that stand on either side,—
The staring boys, a face to every desk,
Bright, dull, pale, blooming, common, picturesque.
Grave is the Master's look; his forehead wears
Thick rows of wrinkles, prints of worrying cares;
Uneasy lie the heads of all that rule,
His most of all whose kingdom is a school.
Supreme he sits; before the awful frown
That bends his brows the boldest eye goes down;
Not more submissive Israel heard and saw
At Sinai's foot the Giver of the Law.

Less stern he seems, who sits in equal Mate
On the twin throne and shares the empire's weight;
Around his lips the subtle life that plays
Steals quaintly forth in many a jesting phrase;
A lightsome nature, not so hard to chafe,
Pleasant when pleased; rough-handled, not so safe;
Some tingling memories vaguely I recall,
But to forgive him. God forgive us all!

One yet remains, whose well-remembered name
Pleads in my grateful heart its tender claim;
His was the charm magnetic, the bright look
That sheds its sunshine on the dreariest book;
A loving soul to every task he brought
That sweetly mingled with the lore he taught;
Sprung from a saintly race that never could
From youth to age be anything but good,
His few brief years in holiest labors spent,
Earth lost too soon the treasure heaven had lent.
Kindest of teachers, studious to divine
Some hint of promise in my earliest line,
These faint and faltering words thou canst not hear
Throb from a heart that holds thy memory dear.
As to the traveller's eye the varied plain
Shows through the window of the flying train,
A mingled landscape, rather felt than seen,
A gravelly bank, a sudden flash of green,
A tangled wood, a glittering stream that flows
Through the cleft summit where the cliff once rose,
All strangely blended in a hurried gleam,
Rock, wood, waste, meadow, village, hill-side, stream, —
So, as we look behind us, life appears,
Seen through the vista of our bygone years.
Yet in the dead past's shadow-filled domain,
Some vanished shapes the hues of life retain;
Unbidden, oft, before our dreaming eyes
From the vague mists in memory's path they rise.
So comes his blooming image to my view,

The friend of joyous days when life was new,
Hope yet untamed, the blood of youth unchilled,
No blank arrear of promise unfulfilled,
Life's flower yet hidden in its sheltering fold,
Its pictured canvas yet to be unrolled.
His the frank smile I vainly look to greet,
His the warm grasp my clasping hand should meet;
How would our lips renew their school-boy talk,
Our feet retrace the old familiar walk!
For thee no more earth's cheerful morning shines
Through the green fringes of the tented pines;
Ah me! is heaven so far thou canst not hear,
Or is thy viewless spirit hovering near,
A fair young presence, bright with morning's glow,
The fresh-cheeked boy of fifty years ago?
Yes, fifty years, with all their circling suns,
Behind them all my glance reverted runs;
Where now that time remote, its griefs, its joys,
Where are its gray-haired men, its bright-haired boys?
Where is the patriarch time could hardly tire,—
The good old, wrinkled, immemorial "squire "?
(An honest treasurer, like a black-plumed swan,
Not every day our eyes may look upon.)
Where the tough champion who, with Calvin's sword,
In wordy conflicts battled for the Lord?
Where the grave scholar, lonely, calm, austere,
Whose voice like music charmed the listening ear,
Whose light rekindled, like the morning star
Still shines upon us through the gates ajar?
Where the still, solemn, weary, sad-eyed man,
Whose care-worn face and wandering eyes would scan,—
His features wasted in the lingering strife
With the pale foe that drains the student's life?
Where my old friend, the scholar, teacher, saint,
Whose creed, some hinted, showed a speck of taint;
He broached his own opinion, which is not
Lightly to be forgiven or forgot;
Some riddle's point,—I scarce remember now,—
Homoi-, perhaps, where they said homo-ou.

(If the unlettered greatly wish to know
Where lies the difference betwixt oi and o,
Those of the curious who have time may search
Among the stale conundrums of their church.)
Beneath his roof his peaceful life I shared,
And for his modes of faith I little cared, —
I, taught to judge men's dogmas by their deeds,
Long ere the days of india-rubber creeds.

Why should we look one common faith to find,
Where one in every score is color-blind?
If here on earth they know not red from green,
Will they see better into things unseen!
Once more to time's old graveyard I return
And scrape the moss from memory's pictured urn.
Who, in these days when all things go by steam,
Recalls the stage-coach with its four-horse team?
Its sturdy driver, — who remembers him?
Or the old landlord, saturnine and grim,
Who left our hill-top for a new abode
And reared his sign-post farther down the road?
Still in the waters of the dark Shawshine
Do the young bathers splash and think they're clean?
Do pilgrims find their way to Indian Ridge,
Or journey onward to the far-off bridge,
And bring to younger ears the story back
Of the broad stream, the mighty Merrimac?
Are there still truant feet that stray beyond
These circling bounds to Pomp's or Haggett's Pond,
Or where the legendary name recalls
The forest's earlier tenant, — "Deerjump Falls"?
Yes, every nook these youthful feet explore,
Just as our sires and grand sires did of yore;
So all life's opening paths, where nature led
Their father's feet, the children's children tread.
Roll the round century's fivescore years away,
Call from our storied past that earliest day
When great Eliphalet (I can see him now, —

Big name, big frame, big voice, and beetling brow),
Then young Eliphalet,—ruled the rows of boys
In homespun gray or old-world corduroys,—
And save for fashion's whims, the benches show
The self-same youths, the very boys we know.
Time works strange marvels: since I trod the green
And swung the gates, what wonders I have seen!
But come what will,—the sky itself may fall,—
As things of course the boy accepts them all.
The prophet's chariot, drawn by steeds of flame,
For daily use our travelling millions claim;
The face we love a sunbeam makes our own;
No more the surgeon hears the sufferer's groan;
What unwrit histories wrapped in darkness lay
Till shovelling Schliemann bared them to the day!
Your Richelieu says, and says it well, my lord,
The pen is (sometimes) mightier than the sword;
Great is the goosequill, say we all; Amen!
Sometimes the spade is mightier than the pen;
It shows where Babel's terraced walls were raised,
The slabs that cracked when Nimrod's palace blazed,
Unearths Mycenee, rediscovers Troy,—
Calmly he listens, that immortal boy.
A new Prometheus tips our wands with fire,
A mightier Orpheus strains the whispering wire,
Whose lightning thrills the lazy winds outrun
And hold the hours as Joshua stayed the sun,—
So swift, in truth, we hardly find a place
For those dim fictions known as time and space.
Still a new miracle each year supplies,—
See at his work the chemist of the skies,
Who questions Sirius in his tortured rays
And steals the secret of the solar blaze;
Hush! while the window-rattling bugles play
The nation's airs a hundred miles away!
That wicked phonograph! hark! how it swears!
Turn it again and make it say its prayers!
And was it true, then, what the story said
Of Oxford's friar and his brazen head?

While wondering Science stands, herself perplexed
At each day's miracle, and asks "What next?"
The immortal boy, the coming heir of all,
Springs from his desk to "urge the flying ball,"
Cleaves with his bending oar the glassy waves,
With sinewy arm the dashing current braves,
The same bright creature in these haunts of ours
That Eton shadowed with her "antique towers."

Boy! Where is he? the long-limbed youth inquires,
Whom his rough chin with manly pride inspires;
Ah, when the ruddy cheek no longer glows,
When the bright hair is white as winter snows,
When the dim eye has lost its lambent flame,
Sweet to his ear will be his school-boy name
Nor think the difference mighty as it seems
Between life's morning and its evening dreams;
Fourscore, like twenty, has its tasks and toys;
In earth's wide school-house all are girls and boys.

Brothers, forgive my wayward fancy. Who
Can guess beforehand what his pen will do?
Too light my strain for listeners such as these,
Whom graver thoughts and soberer speech shall please.
Is he not here whose breath of holy song
Has raised the downcast eyes of Faith so long?
Are they not here, the strangers in your gates,
For whom the wearied ear impatient waits, —
The large-brained scholars whom their toils release, —
The bannered heralds of the Prince of Peace?

Such was the gentle friend whose youth unblamed
In years long past our student-benches claimed;
Whose name, illumined on the sacred page,
Lives in the labors of his riper age;
Such he whose record time's destroying march
Leaves uneffaced on Zion's springing arch

Not to the scanty phrase of measured song,
Cramped in its fetters, names like these belong;
One ray they lend to gild my slender line, —
Their praise I leave to sweeter lips than mine.

Homes of our sires, where Learning's temple rose,
While yet they struggled with their banded foes,
As in the West thy century's sun descends,
One parting gleam its dying radiance lends.
Darker and deeper though the shadows fall
From the gray towers on Doubting Castle's wall,
Though Pope and Pagan re-array their hosts,
And her new armor youthful Science boasts,
Truth, for whose altar rose this holy shrine,
Shall fly for refuge to these bowers of thine;
No past shall chain her with its rusted vow,
No Jew's phylactery bind her Christian brow,
But Faith shall smile to find her sister free,
And nobler manhood draw its life from thee.

Long as the arching skies above thee spread,
As on thy groves the dews of heaven are shed,
With currents widening still from year to year,
And deepening channels, calm, untroubled, clear,
Flow the twin streamlets from thy sacred hill —
Pieria's fount and Siloam's shaded rill!

THE SILENT MELODY

"BRING me my broken harp," he said;
"We both are wrecks, — but as ye will, —
Though all its ringing tones have fled,
Their echoes linger round it still;

It had some golden strings, I know,
But that was long—how long!—ago.

"I cannot see its tarnished gold,
I cannot hear its vanished tone,
Scarce can my trembling fingers hold
The pillared frame so long their own;
We both are wrecks,—a while ago
It had some silver strings, I know,

"But on them Time too long has played
The solemn strain that knows no change,
And where of old my fingers strayed
The chords they find are new and strange,—
Yes! iron strings,—I know,—I know,—
We both are wrecks of long ago.

"We both are wrecks,—a shattered pair,—
Strange to ourselves in time's disguise.
What say ye to the lovesick air
That brought the tears from Marian's eyes?
Ay! trust me,—under breasts of snow
Hearts could be melted long ago!

"Or will ye hear the storm-song's crash
That from his dreams the soldier woke,
And bade him face the lightning flash
When battle's cloud in thunder broke? . . .
Wrecks,—nought but wrecks!—the time was when
We two were worth a thousand men!"

And so the broken harp they bring
With pitying smiles that none could blame;
Alas! there's not a single string
Of all that filled the tarnished frame!
But see! like children overjoyed,

His fingers rambling through the void!

"I clasp thee! Ay . . . mine ancient lyre . . .
Nay, guide my wandering fingers. . . There
They love to dally with the wire
As Isaac played with Esau's hair.
Hush! ye shall hear the famous tune
That Marian called the Breath of June!"

And so they softly gather round
Rapt in his tuneful trance he seems
His fingers move: but not a sound!
A silence like the song of dreams. . . .
"There! ye have heard the air," he cries,
"That brought the tears from Marian's eyes!"

Ah, smile not at his fond conceit,
Nor deem his fancy wrought in vain;
To him the unreal sounds are sweet,—
No discord mars the silent strain
Scored on life's latest, starlit page—
The voiceless melody of age.

Sweet are the lips, of all that sing,
When Nature's music breathes unsought,
But never yet could voice or string
So truly shape our tenderest thought
As when by life's decaying fire
Our fingers sweep the stringless lyre!

OUR HOME — OUR COUNTRY

**FOR THE SEMI-CENTENNIAL CELEBRATION OF THE SET-
TLEMENT OF CAMBRIDGE, MASS., DECEMBER 28, 1880**

YOUR home was mine, — kind Nature's gift;
My love no years can chill;
In vain their flakes the storm-winds sift,
The snow-drop hides beneath the drift,
A living blossom still.

Mute are a hundred long-famed lyres,
Hushed all their golden strings;
One lay the coldest bosom fires,
One song, one only, never tires
While sweet-voiced memory sings.

No spot so lone but echo knows
That dear familiar strain;
In tropic isles, on arctic snows,
Through burning lips its music flows
And rings its fond refrain.

From Pisa's tower my straining sight
Roamed wandering leagues away,
When lo! a frigate's banner bright,
The starry blue, the red, the white,
In far Livorno's bay.

Hot leaps the life-blood from my heart,
Forth springs the sudden tear;
The ship that rocks by yonder mart
Is of my land, my life, a part, —
Home, home, sweet home, is here!

Fades from my view the sunlit scene, —
My vision spans the waves;

I see the elm-encircled green,
The tower, — the steeple, — and, between,
The field of ancient graves.

There runs the path my feet would tread
When first they learned to stray;
There stands the gambrel roof that spread
Its quaint old angles o'er my head
When first I saw the day.

The sounds that met my boyish ear
My inward sense salute, —
The woodnotes wild I loved to hear, —
The robin's challenge, sharp and clear, —
The breath of evening's flute.

The faces loved from cradle days, —
Unseen, alas, how long!
As fond remembrance round them plays,
Touched with its softening moonlight rays,
Through fancy's portal throng.

And see! as if the opening skies
Some angel form had spared
Us wingless mortals to surprise,
The little maid with light-blue eyes,
White necked and golden haired!

. . . .

So rose the picture full in view
I paint in feebler song;
Such power the seamless banner knew
Of red and white and starry blue
For exiles banished long.

Oh, boys, dear boys, who wait as men
To guard its heaven-bright folds,
Blest are the eyes that see again
That banner, seamless now, as then, —
The fairest earth beholds!

Sweet was the Tuscan air and soft
In that unfading hour,
And fancy leads my footsteps oft
Up the round galleries, high aloft
On Pisa's threatening tower.

And still in Memory's holiest shrine
I read with pride and joy,
"For me those stars of empire shine;
That empire's dearest home is mine;
I am a Cambridge boy!"

POEM

AT THE CENTENNIAL ANNIVERSARY DINNER OF THE MASSACHUSETTS MEDICAL SOCIETY, JUNE 8, 1881

THREE paths there be where Learning's favored sons,
Trained in the schools which hold her favored ones,
Follow their several stars with separate aim;
Each has its honors, each its special claim.
Bred in the fruitful cradle of the East,
First, as of oldest lineage, comes the Priest;
The Lawyer next, in wordy conflict strong,
Full armed to battle for the right, — or wrong;
Last, he whose calling finds its voice in deeds,

Frail Nature's helper in her sharpest needs.

Each has his gifts, his losses and his gains,
Each his own share of pleasures and of pains;
No life-long aim with steadfast eye pursued
Finds a smooth pathway all with roses strewed;
Trouble belongs to man of woman born, —
Tread where he may, his foot will find its thorn.

Of all the guests at life's perennial feast,
Who of her children sits above the Priest?
For him the broidered robe, the carven seat,
Pride at his beck, and beauty at his feet,
For him the incense fumes, the wine is poured,
Himself a God, adoring and adored!
His the first welcome when our hearts rejoice,
His in our dying ear the latest voice,
Font, altar, grave, his steps on all attend,
Our staff, our stay, our all but heavenly friend!

Where is the meddling hand that dares to probe
The secret grief beneath his sable robe?
How grave his port! how every gesture tells
Here truth abides, here peace forever dwells;
Vex not his lofty soul with comments vain;
Faith asks no questions; silence, ye profane!

Alas! too oft while all is calm without
The stormy spirit wars with endless doubt;
This is the mocking spectre, scarce concealed
Behind tradition's bruised and battered shield.
He sees the sleepless critic, age by age,
Scrawl his new readings on the hallowed page,
The wondrous deeds that priests and prophets saw
Dissolved in legend, crystallized in law,
And on the soil where saints and martyrs trod
Altars new builded to the Unknown God;

His shrines imperilled, his evangels torn, —
He dares not limp, but ah! how sharp his thorn!

Yet while God's herald questions as he reads
The outworn dogmas of his ancient creeds,
Drops from his ritual the exploded verse,
Blots from its page the Athanasian curse,
Though by the critic's dangerous art perplexed,
His holy life is Heaven's unquestioned text;
That shining guidance doubt can never mar, —
The pillar's flame, the light of Bethlehem's star!

Strong is the moral blister that will draw
Laid on the conscience of the Man of Law
Whom blindfold Justice lends her eyes to see
Truth in the scale that holds his promised fee.
What! Has not every lie its truthful side,
Its honest fraction, not to be denied?
Per contra, — ask the moralist, — in sooth
Has not a lie its share in every truth?
Then what forbids an honest man to try
To find the truth that lurks in every lie,
And just as fairly call on truth to yield
The lying fraction in its breast concealed?
So the worst rogue shall claim a ready friend
His modest virtues boldly to defend,
And he who shows the record of a saint
See himself blacker than the devil could paint.

What struggles to his captive soul belong
Who loves the right, yet combats for the wrong,
Who fights the battle he would fain refuse,
And wins, well knowing that he ought to lose,
Who speaks with glowing lips and look sincere
In spangled words that make the worse appear
The better reason; who, behind his mask,

Hides his true self and blushes at his task,—
What quips, what quillets cheat the inward scorn
That mocks such triumph? Has he not his thorn?

Yet stay thy judgment; were thy life the prize,
Thy death the forfeit, would thy cynic eyes
See fault in him who bravely dares defend
The cause forlorn, the wretch without a friend
Nay, though the rightful side is wisdom's choice,
Wrong has its rights and claims a champion's voice;
Let the strong arm be lifted for the weak,
For the dumb lips the fluent pleader speak;—
When with warm "rebel" blood our street was dyed
Who took, unawed, the hated hirelings' side?
No greener civic wreath can Adams claim,
No brighter page the youthful Quincy's name!

How blest is he who knows no meaner strife
Than Art's long battle with the foes of life!
No doubt assails him, doing still his best,
And trusting kindly Nature for the rest;
No mocking conscience tears the thin disguise
That wraps his breast, and tells him that he lies.
He comes: the languid sufferer lifts his head
And smiles a welcome from his weary bed;
He speaks: what music like the tones that tell,
"Past is the hour of danger,—all is well!"
How can he feel the petty stings of grief
Whose cheering presence always brings relief?
What ugly dreams can trouble his repose
Who yields himself to soothe another's woes?

Hour after hour the busy day has found
The good physician on his lonely round;
Mansion and hovel, low and lofty door,
He knows, his journeys every path explore,—

Where the cold blast has struck with deadly chill
The sturdy dweller on the storm-swept hill,
Where by the stagnant marsh the sickening gale
Has blanched the poisoned tenants of the vale,
Where crushed and maimed the bleeding victim lies,
Where madness raves, where melancholy sighs,
And where the solemn whisper tells too plain
That all his science, all his art, were vain.

How sweet his fireside when the day is done
And cares have vanished with the setting sun!
Evening at last its hour of respite brings
And on his couch his weary length he flings.
Soft be thy pillow, servant of mankind,
Lulled by an opiate Art could never find;
Sweet be thy slumber,—thou hast earned it well,—
Pleasant thy dreams! Clang! goes the midnight bell!

Darkness and storm! the home is far away
That waits his coming ere the break of day;
The snow-clad pines their wintry plumage toss,—
Doubtful the frozen stream his road must cross;
Deep lie the drifts, the slanted heaps have shut
The hardy woodman in his mountain hut,—
Why should thy softer frame the tempest brave?
Hast thou no life, no health, to lose or save?
Look! read the answer in his patient eyes,—
For him no other voice when suffering cries;
Deaf to the gale that all around him blows,
A feeble whisper calls him,—and he goes.

Or seek the crowded city,—summer's heat
Glares burning, blinding, in the narrow street,
Still, noisome, deadly, sleeps the envenomed air,
Unstirred the yellow flag that says "Beware!"
Tempt not thy fate,—one little moment's breath
Bears on its viewless wing the seeds of death;

Thou at whose door the gilded chariots stand,
Whose dear-bought skill unclasps the miser's hand,
Turn from thy fatal quest, nor cast away
That life so precious; let a meaner prey
Feed the destroyer's hunger; live to bless
Those happier homes that need thy care no less!

Smiling he listens; has he then a charm
Whose magic virtues peril can disarm?
No safeguard his; no amulet he wears,
Too well he knows that Nature never spares
Her truest servant, powerless to defend
From her own weapons her unshrinking friend.
He dares the fate the bravest well might shun,
Nor asks reward save only Heaven's "Well done!"

Such are the toils, the perils that he knows,
Days without rest and nights without repose,
Yet all unheeded for the love he bears
His art, his kind, whose every grief he shares.

Harder than these to know how small the part
Nature's proud empire yields to striving Art;
How, as the tide that rolls around the sphere
Laughs at the mounds that delving arms uprear, —
Spares some few roods of oozy earth, but still
Wastes and rebuilds the planet at its will,
Comes at its ordered season, night or noon,
Led by the silver magnet of the moon, —
So life's vast tide forever comes and goes,
Unchecked, resistless, as it ebbs and flows.

Hardest of all, when Art has done her best,
To find the cuckoo brooding in her nest;
The shrewd adventurer, fresh from parts unknown,
Kills off the patients Science thought her own;
Towns from a nostrum-vender get their name,

Fences and walls the cure-all drug proclaim,
Plasters and pads the willing world beguile,
Fair Lydia greets us with astringent smile,
Munchausen's fellow-countryman unlocks
His new Pandora's globule-holding box,
And as King George inquired, with puzzled grin,
"How — how the devil get the apple in?"
So we ask how, — with wonder-opening eyes, —
Such pygmy pills can hold such giant lies!

Yes, sharp the trials, stern the daily tasks
That suffering Nature from her servant asks;
His the kind office dainty menials scorn,
His path how hard, — at every step a thorn!
What does his saddening, restless slavery buy?
What save a right to live, a chance to die, —
To live companion of disease and pain,
To die by poisoned shafts untimely slain?

Answer from hoary eld, majestic shades, —
From Memphian courts, from Delphic colonnades,
Speak in the tones that Persia's despot heard
When nations treasured every golden word
The wandering echoes wafted o'er the seas,
From the far isle that held Hippocrates;
And thou, best gift that Pergamus could send
Imperial Rome, her noblest Caesar's friend,
Master of masters, whose unchallenged sway
Not bold Vesalius dared to disobey;
Ye who while prophets dreamed of dawning times
Taught your rude lessons in Salerno's rhymes,
And ye, the nearer sires, to whom we owe
The better share of all the best we know,
In every land an ever-growing train,
Since wakening Science broke her rusted chain, —
Speak from the past, and say what prize was sent
To crown the toiling years so freely spent!

List while they speak:
        In life's uneven road
Our willing hands have eased our brothers' load;
One forehead smoothed, one pang of torture less,
One peaceful hour a sufferer's couch to bless,
The smile brought back to fever's parching lips,
The light restored to reason in eclipse,
Life's treasure rescued like a burning brand
Snatched from the dread destroyer's wasteful hand;
Such were our simple records day by day,
For gains like these we wore our lives away.
In toilsome paths our daily bread we sought,
But bread from heaven attending angels brought;
Pain was our teacher, speaking to the heart,
Mother of pity, nurse of pitying art;
Our lesson learned, we reached the peaceful shore
Where the pale sufferer asks our aid no more,—
These gracious words our welcome, our reward
Ye served your brothers; ye have served your Lord!

RHYMES OF A LIFE-TIME

FROM the first gleam of morning to the gray
Of peaceful evening, lo, a life unrolled!
In woven pictures all its changes told,
Its lights, its shadows, every flitting ray,
Till the long curtain, falling, dims the day,
Steals from the dial's disk the sunlight's gold,
And all the graven hours grow dark and cold
Where late the glowing blaze of noontide lay.
Ah! the warm blood runs wild in youthful veins,—
Let me no longer play with painted fire;
New songs for new-born days! I would not tire
The listening ears that wait for fresher strains

In phrase new-moulded, new-forged rhythmic chains,
With plaintive measures from a worn-out lyre.
August 2, 1881.